Turkey Surprise

The gopher hole

The pond

Turkey Surprise

Peggy Archer

illustrated by **Thor Wickstrom**

PUFFIN BOOKS

Two pilgrim brothers sang as they walked down the path together.

"*We're two mighty pilgrims*
coming your way.
Looking for a turkey
for Thanksgiving Day.
We'll pluck him, and stuff him,
and cook him up right.
We'll gobble, gobble turkey
for dinner tonight!"

The little pilgrim thought about plucking and stuffing. He thought about cooking.

He wasn't so sure about plucking and stuffing and cooking.

He wasn't so sure about having a turkey for Thanksgiving dinner.

"The first turkey we see will be Thanksgiving dinner," said the big pilgrim.

The little pilgrim looked through his spyglass. "But what if we don't *see* any turkeys?" he asked.

"Don't worry," said the big pilgrim. "We will."

Around the bend, a turkey was in a tizzy! "The pilgrim brothers are coming!" he cried. "If they see me, they'll pluck out all my feathers, stuff me with bread crumbs, and cook me for Thanksgiving dinner. Where, oh where, can I hide?"

"Turkey," a bird called, "fly up here in this tree. The leaves will hide you."

He flew up into the tree.

He flapped his wings.

The turkey took a running start.

Then, *Whoosh!* A breeze climbed into the air. It blew the dry leaves right off the tree.

"Oh, no," cried the turkey. "Here come the pilgrim brothers!"

The little pilgrim looked through his spyglass. He saw a tree with its leaves on the ground. He saw something in the tree.

"I'm tired of turkey for Thanksgiving dinner," the little pilgrim said. "Are you *sure* we want a turkey?"

"Well," the big pilgrim said, "*Father* wants a turkey."

"Come on," the little pilgrim said. "Let's go this way." And off they went in another direction, singing:

"We're two mighty pilgrims
coming your way.
Looking for a turkey
for Thanksgiving Day.
We'll pluck him, and stuff him,
and cook him up right.
We'll gobble, gobble turkey
for dinner tonight!"

"Come on," the little pilgrim said. "Let's go this way." And off they went, in a new direction, singing:

"We're two mighty pilgrims
coming your way.
Looking for a turkey
for Thanksgiving Day.
We'll pluck him, and stuff him,
and cook him up right.
We'll gobble, gobble turkey
for dinner tonight!"

The little pilgrim looked through his spyglass. He saw a gopher hole. He saw something sitting next to the gopher hole.

"I never really liked turkey," the little pilgrim said. "Are you *really* sure we want a turkey for Thanksgiving dinner?"

"Well," the big pilgrim said, "*Mother* wants a turkey."

"You can hide in a hole in the ground like me," the gopher said.

He jumped into his gopher hole. The turkey dove in after him.

His head went in. His neck went in. But the rest of him would not go in.

"Oh, help," cried the turkey. "I'm stuck! Now what will I do?"

"Don't worry," said the gopher. From inside his gopher hole, he pushed and pushed.

Pop! The turkey fell backward onto the ground.

"Oh, dear!" cried the turkey. "Here come the pilgrim brothers!"

The turkey ran the other way. He saw a gopher sitting in the grass.

"The pilgrim brothers are coming!" the turkey cried. "If they see me, they will pluck out all my feathers, stuff me with bread crumbs, and cook me for Thanksgiving dinner. Where, oh where, can I hide?"

The turkey ran the other way. He came to a pond. A fish was swimming in circles.

"Oh, Fish!" the turkey cried. "The pilgrim brothers are coming. If they see me, they will pluck out all of my feathers, stuff me with bread crumbs, and cook me for Thanksgiving dinner. Where, oh where, can I hide?"

"You can hide behind this rock, like me," said the fish. "See? Just jump into the water."

The turkey jumped into the water. *Plop!*

He sank to the bottom of the pond.

Gurgle, gurgle went the water into his eyes and nose.

Cough, cough went the turkey as he pushed himself up.

Splutter, splatter went the water out of the turkey's nose and mouth.

"I just remembered," he said to the fish. "Turkeys can't swim!

And here come the pilgrim brothers!"

The little pilgrim looked through his spyglass. He saw a pond. He saw something big and wet beside the pond.

"Turkey, turkey, turkey," the little pilgrim said. "Is that all anyone has for Thanksgiving dinner?"

"Well, no," the big pilgrim said. "There's corn on the cob, and applesauce, and dessert, too. But Mother and Father want us to bring home a turkey."

"Well," said the little pilgrim. "What if we can't *find* a turkey?"

The big pilgrim thought. "Well, we have to bring *something* home," he said.

The little pilgrim looked through his spyglass again. "I'll meet you at the pumpkin patch," he said.

The big pilgrim went to the pumpkin patch. The little pilgrim went to the pond. He came face-to-face with the turkey.

"Come on!" he said to the turkey. "You can hide behind the woodpile, like I do."

The turkey trembled.

"Quick," said the little pilgrim. "Before my brother sees you!"

The turkey ducked behind the woodpile. The little pilgrim smiled.

He went to find his brother.

"What a good Thanksgiving dinner we will bring home!" he said.

The two pilgrim brothers walked down the path together. They carried a heavy pumpkin between them. They sang,

"We're two mighty pilgrims
coming your way.
Bringing home a feast
for Thanksgiving Day.
Turkey sounds good
all stuffed with bread.
But we'd rather gobble, gobble
pumpkin pie instead!"

To Chuck, and all the gobblers who followed—
Kathy, Brian, Kevin, Dan, Megan, and Sarah
—P. A.

To my Scandinavian brothers, Matti and Lennart
—T. W.

PUFFIN BOOKS • Published by the Penguin Group • Penguin Young Readers Group, 345 Hudson Street, New York, New York 10014, U.S.A. • Penguin Group (Canada), 90 Eglinton Avenue East, Suite 700, Toronto, Ontario, Canada M4P 2Y3 (a division of Pearson Penguin Canada Inc.) • Penguin Books Ltd, 80 Strand, London WC2R 0RL, England • Penguin Ireland, 25 St Stephen's Green, Dublin 2, Ireland (a division of Penguin Books Ltd) • Penguin Group (Australia), 250 Camberwell Road, Camberwell, Victoria 3124, Australia (a division of Pearson Australia Group Pty Ltd) • Penguin Books India Pvt Ltd, 11 Community Centre, Panchsheel Park, New Delhi-110 017, India • Penguin Group (NZ), Cnr Airborne and Rosedale Roads, Albany, Auckland 1310, New Zealand (a division of Pearson New Zealand Ltd) • Penguin Books (South Africa) (Pty) Ltd, 24 Sturdee Avenue, Rosebank, Johannesburg 2196, South Africa

Registered Offices: Penguin Books Ltd, 80 Strand, London WC2R 0RL, England

First published in the United States of America by Dial Books for Young Readers, a division of Penguin Young Readers Group, 2005 • Published by Puffin Books, a division of Penguin Young Readers Group, 2007

1 2 3 4 5 6 7 8 9 10

Text copyright © Peggy Archer, 2005 • Pictures copyright © Thor Wickstrom, 2005 • All rights reserved

THE LIBRARY OF CONGRESS HAS CATALOGED THE DIAL BOOKS FOR YOUNG READERS EDITION AS FOLLOWS:
Archer, Peggy. • Turkey surprise / Peggy Archer ; illustrated by Thor Wickstrom. • p. cm. • Summary: A turkey hides from two brothers looking for food for Thanksgiving Day, and they end up finding something better to eat. • ISBN: 0-8037-2969-3 (hc) • [1. Thanksgiving Day—Fiction. 2. Turkeys—Fiction. 3. Brothers—Fiction.] • I. Wickstrom, Thor, ill. II. Title. • PZ7.A6749Tu 2005 [E]—dc22 2004003397

Puffin Books ISBN 978-0-14-240852-0

Printed in China • Designed by Jasmin Rubero • Text set in Bookman

DATE DUE

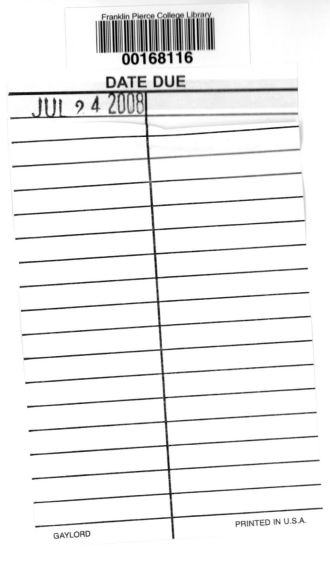

JUL 2 4 2008

GAYLORD

PRINTED IN U.S.A.